Billy Buttons

Billy Bob Buttons is a young talented author. On top of being a secondary school English teacher, he is also a pilot.

He is the author of the much loved, The Gullfoss Legends, Rubery Award finalist, Felicity Brady and the Wizard's Bookshop, UK People's Book Prize runner-up, TOR Assassin Hunter, TOR Wolf Rising and the best-selling, I Think I Murdered Miss.

Muffin Monster is his tenth children's novel.

When not writing, he enjoys tennis and playing 'MONSTER!' with his three children.

For my little Albert and the
grandad he never met

The Wishing Shelf Press, www.bbbuttons.co.uk

Copyright Edward H Trayer

ISBN 978 0 9574767 90

Cover by Elizabeth Spooner

Drawings from www.ArtOnTheWeb.com

Contents

Chapter 1

A Very Odd Letter

ALBERT SAT ON THE BUS WATCHING the tiny town of Trotswood rumble by. He was very excited. He was going to stay with Grandad and Grandma for two weeks and help them in their muffin shop.

Nobody in his family, not even his mum and dad, had been invited to Grandad's shop for months and months and MONTHS and nobody knew why. So he had been over the moon when Mum had shown him the letter.

But, to be honest, he'd been a bit sad too. So, yesterday, he and his mum had snuggled up on the sofa, watched cartoons on TV and gobbled popcorn. He'd felt much better after that.

As the bus thundered and swerved up the tiny, cobbled street, Albert pulled the crumpled scrap of paper from his bag and unfolded it.

Hello Albert,
Your grandma and I were wondering
if you fancy spending two weeks with

Muffin Monster

us this summer. We miss you very much
and there's a tiny problem I think you
can help me with.

Let me know and I will pick you up
from the bus stop.

Love,

Grandad Irish

PS

VERY IMPORTANT! Bring your cycling

helmet.

PPS

And your football shinpads.

Everybody, even the postman and
the newspaper boy, called Grandad,
Grandad Irish. He was from Dublin, you
see, and he always had a fresh clover
pinned to his lapel.

The bus turned a corner, trundling by
a shaggy-looking dog peeing up a
tree. Albert wondered what the
problem was. Was Grandma ill and

Muffin Monster

Grandad needed help in the kitchen baking all the muffins? He knew the shop was often busy in the summer. But why the helmet and shinpads, he pondered, and why did Grandad not ask him to bring his bicycle and football too.

Albert spotted there were lots of gummy-looking red blobs on the bottom corner of the letter. He put the biggest of them up to his nose and sniffed. 'Hmm!' Strawberry jam with a tiny hint of rhubarb.

His tummy rumbled as he thought of Magic Muffins, his grandad's cosy little shop. There were hazelnut muffins, rhubarb muffins, even muffins crammed with toffee chunks; and every muffin, EVERY MUFFIN was topped with jam and a tasty red cherry.

Suddenly, the bus shuddered and rolled to a stop. Excitedly, Albert stuffed the letter back in his bag, thanked the driver and jumped off.

Shading his eyes from the afternoon sun, he soon spotted Grandad Irish sitting on a graffiti-scrawled bench under a conker tree. 'Hello!' Albert yelled, sprinting over to him. He was a very fast runner.

Grandad stood up slowly and waved. He was a rather odd-looking fellow. He always, ALWAYS had on

Muffin Monster

a brown, patched-up jumper and very old slippers on his dolphin-flippered feet. His grey, wispy curls were often hidden under a bobbly hat (even when he was in the shop) and he only had two teeth. Just two. He had lost

the rest of them in a cricket match.
'Mind you, I did catch the ball,' he
always told Albert with a playful wink.
'Just not with my hands.'

Grandad dropped to a knee and
hugged the grinning boy. Then, he took
him by the shoulders and asked him,
sternly, 'Where's your helmet and
shinpads, lad?'

Chapter 2
Rufus Splinter

AFTER PULLING HIS CYCLING HELMET and Manchester United shinpads from his bag and showing them to his grandad, they set off on foot to the muffin shop.

'I did plan to pick you up in the old delivery van,' mumbled Grandad apologetically, 'but my eyesight's not what it was.'

But Albert was happy to walk. Grandad's VW camper van was almost as old as Grandad himself and only went 20mph. On a good day. Over a cliff! It was always backfiring too, scaring the bejeepers out of any unsuspecting cats and dogs and frightening away all the birds in the trees.

Albert shrugged and patted the old man's arm. 'It's OK. I enjoy a stroll.' He hoped this wasn't the tiny problem Grandad had referred to in his letter. Albert was only eight years old; way too young to be driving an exploding van!

Struggling up a hill, Grandad glanced over at Albert. 'You grew a lot over the spring,' he panted. 'It must be all the sun.' He winked playfully at the boy.

Albert grinned and nodded. He WAS a tall boy; skinny too, so the kids in school called him Lollipop. But it didn't bother him. Better than Teeny-Tiny, Ugly-Wuggly. Janet Doogan in Class Three was called that; poor girl. Anyway, it was fun being tall. No jar was too high for his fingertips and he was by far the best player in the basketball club.

Strolling up the bustling High Street,

Albert saw there were lots of new
shops. A barbers, a DIY shop full of
hammers and screwdrivers, even a
shop selling nothing but shiny, new
Hoovers. Albert spotted there was a
sign taped to the window.

The Most
Powerful Hoover
In The World

Intrigued, he ambled over and
gazed in. There, sitting on a low shelf,
was a long, silver, bullet-shaped

canister with a nozzle poking out of the end. It was almost the size of a desk and etched in the shiny metal were the words

MegaSucker

2000 Turbo

'Looks as if it'd suck up a cow,' murmured Grandad, who had walked over too.

Albert chuckled. Then, turning away from the window, he spotted another new shop.

He stared at it in horror. 'Grandad!' he howled, waving his hands frantically. 'Over there! There's a muffin shop.'

The old man scowled and nodded, looking to his feet. 'Yes, I know,' he muttered dourly.

It looked much bigger than Magic Muffins with a steel roof and a revolving glass door. There were lots of muffins in the window but Albert was glad to see they were much smaller than the muffins his grandad sold. Sadly, he saw they cost a lot less too.

Just then, a man with the belly of a pig - who had just scoffed another pig - unjammed himself from the muffin

shop's doorway. 'Wotcha, old timer,'
he called to Grandad, waddling over
to them.

Grandad rolled his eyes. 'Rufus
Splinter,' he muttered. Albert had a
feeling Mr Splinter was not on his
grandad's Christmas card list.

He stopped in front of them, his
balled-up hand full of a half-chewed
banana muffin, his brow crumpled up
in a scowl.

Albert looked at him with interest. He
was very, VERY fat, his bum almost
drooping down to the backs of his
knees. He had tiny, piggy eyes and his
lips and the top half of his chin were
hidden under a bushy, walrus

moustache. He had, Albert thought, the determined look of a hungry fox. Nothing was going to stand in this man's way.

Splinter stepped up to Albert and scowled at him. 'And who's this skinny fellow?'

'I'm Albert,' answered the boy with a matching scowl. 'His grandson.'

'I see.' Splinter sniffed and wiped his piggy snout on his sleeve. He did not seem at all interested in the boy. 'So, old timer,' he turned to Albert's grandad, 'any thoughts on my overly-kind offer?'

The old man stepped back, wrinkling up his nose as if Splinter smelt of rotten eggs. 'Oh, yes.'

'Wonderful!' With a gleeful leer, Splinter stuffed the rest of the muffin in his mouth and rubbed his hands together. 'Go on, then,' he rumbled, grinning wolfishly, 'how much do y' want?'

'The answer is no.'

'NO!' he howled, spitting crumbs on his protruding belly.

'Correct.' Grandpa's jaw stiffened. 'I'd rather jump off a cliff than sell Magic Muffins to a sewer rat.'

'SEWER!' bellowed Splinter. 'RAT!' With his flabby cheeks turning a sort of beetroot-purple, the man glowered at Albert's grandad. 'You old fool,' he sneered. 'You won't last another week.' Then, with a snooty sniff, he stormed off back to his shop.

Albert stared after Splinter's swaying, rhino-sized bottom. 'So he's the, er - tiny problem?' He did not look very tiny to him.

'I only wish,' the old man murmured and, with a sigh, he ambled off too.

They were in the old town now. The street was cobbled and crammed with tiny, ramshankled shops selling silks, kilned pots and tiny clockwork toys.

Trudging by three old women on a bench, one of them called out, 'Is Imelda back yet?'

Imelda, Albert knew, was his

grandma's name.

'Soon,' called back Grandad, hurrying by them. Albert ran to catch him up.

Looking back over his shoulder, he saw the woman was staring after them. She did not look too happy with his grandad's reply.

They plodded by a bakery, Albert wetting his lips to the smell of the pastry; and then by a butcher's shop, pigs dangling in the window. Until, at last, they got to Magic Muffins.

It was a very cosy-looking shop with a crooked, red door and bulging, sloping timbers. It seemed to almost cuddle up to the street, the slanted thatched roof shadowing the sun.

Albert had almost forgotten how wonderful the shop looked, though he spotted there were hardly any muffins in the window and the glass was all grimy and smudged.

A light bulb flicked on in his skull. Now he understood. Grandad needed help fixing things and tidying up.

Thrilled to be back, he followed the old man over to the shop. But when they got to the door, Grandad suddenly clasped his hand on the boy's shoulder. 'Shhh,' he whispered, his two teeth chewing fretfully on his bottom lip.

Puzzled, Albert stood with Grandad

Irish on the street.

The seconds ticked slowly by. 'What's wrong?' ventured Albert at last.

The old man jumped as if he'd forgotten his grandson was even there. 'Nothing! Nothing!' He pulled a shiny key from his pocket. 'Let's go in. Lots of muffins to bake for the morning.'

Albert frowned as he watched him unlock the door. Then, wondering if the old man was going a little potty, he followed him into the muffin shop.

Chapter 3

Jam!

EVERYWHERE!

ALBERT LOVED BEING BACK IN Magic Muffins. It was such a fun shop to be in and full of the most interesting things. Big, steel bowls hung on the kitchen wall and shiny whisks and baking trays hid in the drawers. In the front of the shop there was a wooden bench and, on it, a big, brass cash till, a coffee pot and a big bowl of tooth picks. It was here that Grandad stood for most of the day, selling his cherry-topped muffins.

Albert and his grandad spent all afternoon and most of the evening in the kitchen. They baked lemon muffins, plum, even butterscotch and banana and, soon, the pots, the pans, the whisks and all of the wooden spoons were dripping with jammy goo. Baking with his grandad, thought Albert, licking his fingers and thumbs, was the best fun in the world.

Suddenly, a low growl echoed

through the kitchen.

Albert jumped, almost dropping a tray of newly-baked banana muffins on the floor. 'W-what was that?' he stammered.

'What was what?' asked Grandad Irish calmly.

Albert looked at him in bewilderment. 'That blood-curdling growl!'

'Oh, that,' muttered the old man, tossing a rolling pin in the sink. 'Just my tummy rumbling.' He chuckled but Albert saw him shoot the cellar door a very nervy look. Out of the corner of his eye, the boy spotted there was a chunky-looking padlock on it. What was Grandad hiding down there? A wild dog?

The boy shrugged. 'I'm hungry too,' he agreed.

'Oh my!' Looking sheepishly to his slippers, Grandad rapped his knuckle on his skull. 'I forgot dinner. I'm a very poor host.'

Albert smiled and waved his hand at the hill of warm muffins. 'Shall we try a few then?'

Looking up, Grandad smiled too. 'Well, best to check 'em, hey? We don't want to be selling bad buns, do we?'

He pulled up two wonky-looking stools and together they set about sampling the many different kinds of muffins.

'So, how're your sisters?' Grandad asked him.

'Driving me nuts,' muttered Albert with a roll of his eyes.

The old man chuckled. 'That's what girls do.'

The boy grinned and nodded.

Albert had two older sisters. They were twins and they looked identical in almost every way. Almost. Beatrix had a tiny freckle on her right cheek. Rebecca did not.

'Oh, Grandad,' mumbled Albert, spitting crumbs, 'I forgot to ask. Where's Grandma?'

'Grandma!' coughed Grandad, choking on his rhubarb muffin.

'Yes, you know. Grandma Imelda. Mum's mum. Your, er - wife.'

'Oh, Grandma!' bellowed the old man with a chesty laugh. 'She's, er - on holiday.'

'On holiday!'

'Yes. In Italy. She's visiting her sister there.'

Albert frowned. 'But I thought Grandma's sister lived in Skegness.'

'Oh, yes. Well, er - she's on holiday in Sweden too.'

'Italy.'

'Sorry?'

'I thought Grandma was on holiday in Italy.'

'Yes, yes, Italy. Did I say Egypt?' The old man's cheeks burned crimson. 'Sorry. I'm so forgetful.'

'No, you...' Albert stopped. By then, he was totally confused, but he was way too sleepy to get to the bottom of

Grandad's ramblings tonight.

Yawning, he wiped the muffin crumbs off his jumper. It had been a very long day: travelling all the way here on the bus and baking hundreds and hundreds of muffins. 'When will Grandma be back?' he asked, rubbing his eyes.

But Grandad did not answer and pulled a silver pocket watch from his apron pocket. 'Oh my! Why, it's almost ten o'clock. Off to bed with y', lad. Big day tomorrow. Lots and lots of muffins to sell.'

Albert nodded thankfully. He was feeling very, very sleepy. After hugging Grandad goodnight, he trudged up the steps to his room. Then, after pulling on his pyjamas and brushing his teeth, he snuggled down in his new bed to sleep.

As Albert lay there, he suddenly remembered he'd forgotten to ask Grandad Irish what the tiny problem was. The boy shut his eyes. There was no hurry, he thought. He'd ask him in the morning.

Chapter 4
Munching Muffin Monster

SUDDENLY, ALBERT BOLTED UP IN HIS bed. Wiping his clammy brow, he looked at his watch. It was past midnight. What had woken him, he wondered. Owls hooting? The wind in

the trees?

He remembered he'd been having a
very scary nightmare full of fanged,
furry monsters. His old dog, Poppy, had
been in it too.

Albert felt terribly thirsty so, rubbing
his eyes, he slipped out from under his

warm duvet, put his slippers on the wrong feet and padded down the steps to the hallway. There, to his surprise, he discovered his grandad laying on a blanket by the kitchen door. And he seemed to be fast asleep!

Softly, Albert crept over to him. Oddly, his curls were hidden under a green, steel collinder and a rusty frying pan was roped to his tummy. Even odder, there was a baseball bat laying on his chest.

A muffled, 'Munch! Munch! Munch!' drew Albert's eyes to the kitchen door. What was going on in there, he wondered. Had a burglar broken in and was wolfing down all the muffins they had baked?

Clenching his slippery fists, he slipped by his snoring grandad, pushed open the door and crept in. It was very dark in the kitchen so Albert felt for the lightswitch with his fingertips. Got it! And he flicked on the light…

'Aaaaaaaagh!' Albert bellowed, for there, sitting in the middle of the floor scoffing all the muffins, was a huge, slimy-looking monster. Bigger than a shed, it had gigantic, swirling eyes, long, crooked fingers and teeth the size of a killer shark's.

Albert stared pot lid-eyed at the monster. The monster glared back at

Albert. Then, with a thundery growl, it dropped the muffins to the floor, hopped up on two curly-clawed feet and began to slowly waddle over to him.

Albert wanted to run but his knees felt like jelly and his legs no longer seemed to work.

'OY!' yelled Grandad, rushing into the kitchen, twirling the bat over his collinder helmet. 'STAY AWAY FROM MY GRANDSON, Y' BIG BULLY!'

The monster stopped and, for a second, Albert thought it was going to attack the old man. But, then, with a low growl, it snatched up a tray of plum muffins, twirled like a top and oozed off down the steps to the cellar.

Albert stood there, just - stood there, his mouth as dry as the Sahara desert, his thoughts so jumbled, so - topsy turvy, he did not know what to say. With his chin to his chest, he watched Grandad rush over to the cellar door and slam it shut. Then, slowly, the old man turned to look at him. 'That,' he wheezed, 'is the, er - tiny problem I want you to help me with.'

The boy looked at him in astonishment. 'You call that THING tiny?'

Chapter 5
Monsters Enjoy
Jazz!

THE NEXT MORNING, AFTER A VERY, very, VERY sleepless night, Albert sat in the kitchen with his grandad chomping on a bowl of Sugar Puffs and shooting the cellar door nervy looks. The boy spotted there was now a new, even bigger padlock on it. But was it up to the job of stopping the monster? Remembering his gigantic fangs and razor-sharp claws, Albert very much doubted it.

'Your grandma and I picked him up on holiday in Zimbabwe three years ago,' the old man told his grandson. 'He was just a baby then. The fellow in the shop told us he was a sort of dog.' Frowning, he scratched his bobbly hat with his thumb. 'A Jack Russell, if I remember correctly.'

'A Jack Russell!' echoed Albert with a roll of his eyes. 'Grandad, I suspect he was telling fibs.'

Muffin Monster

The old man shrugged and supped his coffee. 'I must admit, his eyes were very swirly and he did seem a bit, er - mushy. Anyway, to begin with he wasn't much of a problem. We kept him in the cellar, walked him at night and every day we fed him a few muffins. He loved plum the most. But he grew and grew and grew till he was bigger than a bus and scoffing a hundred a day.' Grandad swallowed. 'Then it happened.'

Albert looked up from his brimming bowl. 'What happened?'

'He, er - gobbled up your grandmother.'

Albert's spoon fell in the milk with a

splash and a clank. 'HE GOBBLED UP GRANDMA!'

The old man nodded soberly. 'If you remember, she WAS getting a bit chubby and on the day it happened she had on a very pretty, red dress. I think he thought she was a muffin.'

'A plum muffin,' murmured Albert who was very much in shock. 'So, er - she's not in Italy then?'

'No'

'Or France?' the boy suggested hopefully.

'No.'

'Egypt?'

'She's never even been,' mumbled Grandad with a sheepish look. 'She

went down in the cellar to feed him.
There was a yell. I rushed down there
but all that was left were her slippers.
They were VERY slimy. I put them back
in her bedroom,' he added with a sniff.

Albert did not know what to say. Poor
Grandma, he thought.

'Imelda, bless her, she loved him. He
was her pet. Much better than a cat,
she told me. Always feeding him and
playing him music. It seems monsters, or
this monster anyway, enjoy a spot of
jazz.'

Albert frowned thoughtfully,
drumming his fingers on the table top.
Then, he thumped the wood with his
balled-up hand spilling soggy Sugar

Puffs on his lap. 'Grandad! We must trap the blighter.'

'Trap it!' The old man ballooned his cheeks then, slowly, deflated them. 'But how?'

'I think I know a way but we will need

to go shopping and buy a few things.'
Giving up on the Sugar Puffs, he
grabbed a banana from the bowl. 'But
even if we do trap it, where will we put
it? We can't bring it all the way back to
Zimbabwe.'

His grandad smiled impishly. 'Don't
you worry, lad. I know the perfect spot.'

Chapter 6
Preparing for
Battle

AFTER BRUSHING HIS TEETH AND
switching his pyjamas for grey shorts
and a floppy, v-necked jumper, Albert
went with his grandad to the shops. To
begin with, they went to ASDA, filling

the trolley to overflowing with eggs, plums and pots of raspberry jam. Then they jumped on the Number Six bus and went to Reel It In, a fishing shop at the other end of town. Finally, they popped to the Hoover shop to buy the most important item of all.

When they got back to Magic Muffins, they were very hot and tired, but there was too much to do to rest. They decided to split up, Grandad to begin baking and Albert to set his cunning trap.

It took Albert almost three hours to sort everything: climbing ladders, lugging nets and unravelling balls of string. Then, when he was finally happy with his work, he dashed over to help his grandad.

To bake a dozen or so run-of-the-mill, everyday, plum muffins you need the following:

3 lbs of sugar

4 eggs

2 lbs of flour

Half a jar of jam and six plums

But the muffin they were baking was no run-of-the-mill, everyday muffin. For this muffin, Grandad put in

127 lbs of sugar

211 eggs

Muffin Monster

99 lbs of flour

14 jars of jam and 422 plums

It took Albert and his grandad almost three hours, employing the help of seven wooden spoons and eleven whisks, to mix it properly and when it was finally all fluffed up, they discovered the old bathtub they had put it in was too big to fit in the oven! So they divided it up and baked it in much smaller mop buckets. Then they stuck all the spongy chunks together with the raspberry jam.

The moon was high in the sky when they finally dragged the gigantic muffin over to the cellar door.

'It must be a record,' panted Albert, stepping back and crossing his gangly arms. 'The biggest muffin in all of England.'

'In the world,' Grandad corrected him with a grin.

Albert helter-skeltered up the spiral steps to his room and pulled his shinpads and helmet from his bag. Hastily, he put them on. Then he scampered over to his grandma and grandad's bedroom to fetch Grandma's old record player. Carrying it back down, he set it on the floor next to the muffin.

Grandad plugged it in and gently placed the needle on the spinning record. Trumpet music instantly filled the shop and, a split second later, a low thundery growl erupted from under Albert's feet.

'Is everything set?' whispered Grandad urgently. Albert saw he'd strapped the steel collinder and frying pan back on.

Albert nodded. 'I, er - I think so.' But he had a nasty feeling his plan was not going to work. In fact, he'd rather bet on a pig flying by.

THUMP!

THUMP!

THUMP!

The monster was coming up the cellar steps!

'Hurry!' barked Grandad and, grabbing his grandson's hand, he pulled him from the kitchen.

Chapter 7
The Megasucker
2000 TURBO

GRANDAD PRODDED ALBERT IN THE tummy with his finger. 'Let's get him,' he whispered.

They were knelt in the corridor, on the cold, hard floor, only feet from where the muffin monster was enjoying his dinner.

'No! Not yet,' hissed back the boy, putting a warning hand on the old man's arm. 'Remember, he must gobble up every crumb or my plan won't work.'

MUNCH!

MUNCH!

MUNCH!

Then, suddenly, the munching stopped.

Albert looked slowly up at his grandad. The old man looked slowly back down at Albert.

'Okay,' the boy whispered with a jittery swallow. 'Let's do it.'

Dragging the MegaSucker 2000 Turbo they had got from the Hoover shop, the staggered into the kitchen. There, they discovered the monster sprawled flat on the floor like a sleeping cow, his gigantic belly sprinkled with muffin crumbs.

With a horrible, husky snarl, the monster staggered up. It swayed a little to the left. It swayed a little to the right. Then…

it

slumped

Muffin Monster

back

down!

Albert's super-fantastic plan was working! The monster's belly was so stuffed with plum muffin, he was too fat to stand up.

With a cry of victory, Albert sprinted over to the far wall. There, just over the spoon drawer, a rope hung from the roof. He yanked on it and, almost instantly, a gigantic fishing net fell over the struggling monster.

Fighting to untangle his long limbs,

the monster rumbled and howled, shuddered and growled, but no matter how hard he kicked and no matter how hard he punched, the wiry net held, keeping him pinned firmly to the floor.

With the help of his grandad, Albert dragged the Hoover over to the wriggling monster and switched it on. Then, together, they slammed the tip of the nozzle up to the monster's slimy skin.

The MegaSucker rumbled and howled, shuddered and growled but the muffin monster, well, it just sat there...

Albert's super-fantastic plan was NOT

working!

'TRY THE TURBO BUTTON!' hollered Albert's grandad over the whining motor.

The boy's eyes widened. THE TURBO BUTTON! Why had he not thought of that? Gritting his teeth, he slammed his finger down onto the big, red button. The MegaSucker snarled wildly and jumped in his hands but the boy held on and…

SSSLLLUUURRRppp!

In 3.6 seconds flat, it had

sucked up every morsel of the monster's jelly-like flesh.

'We got it!' gasped Albert, his eyes glued to the juddering MegaSucker. He had a feeling the monster was not enjoying his new home. 'Grandad, I don't think it will hold him for long,' he warned.

But the old man just chuckled - in a very worrying way, Albert thought - and winked impishly. 'I know just where to put the nasty critter,'

They lugged the jumping, jerking, howling MegaSucker along the dark corridor and out of the front door. From there they carted it over to Grandad's VW van.

Muffin Monster

'Good job it's almost midnight and everybody's in bed,' gasped Albert. He was finding it terribly difficult to keep a grip on the twitching MegaSucker. 'Or they'd be calling the cops.' The Hoover jumped wildly in his grasp and he almost dropped it. 'Grandad!' he yelped. 'I gotta stop.'

'Just hold on,' wheezed Grandad, urgently trying to lever open the van door with the tip of his slipper. It was very old and very rusty but, finally, it slid to the left and they tossed the Hoover in the back.

Growls and blood-curdling howls instantly erupted from the van and it began to rock back and forth like a ship in a storm.

'Now what do we do?' huffed Albert, bending over and putting his hands on his knees. He's been so busy setting his trap, he'd totally forgotten to ask what the plan was if they did successfully catch the thing.

'Now we go for a spin.' Grandad yanked a bunch of keys from his pocket and tossed them over to Albert. 'I'm very sorry,' he told the boy, 'but my eyesight's appalling. You'll have to drive.'

Chapter 8

Knocking Over

EVERYTHING!

'NOTHING TO IT, LAD,' GRANDAD
assured him. 'Just turn the key and off
we go.

With a reluctant shrug, the boy
pushed in the key and twisted.

Instantly, a gigantic BANG erupted from the back of the van and the cabin began to fill with a petrol-smelling fog.

'Terribly sorry,' coughed Grandad, rolling down in window. 'Not driven the old banger in months.'

Chewing fretfully on his lower lip, Albert twisted the key for a second time and, thankfully, the motor spluttered into life.

'Foot on the clutch,' Grandad instructed him.

With a deep frown, the boy turned to look at him. 'What's a clutch?' he asked.

'Oh, er - sorry. By your foot. The pedal

on the left.'

Albert nodded and put his boot on it. Instantly, Grandad slammed the van into first and, with a bang and a puff of liquorice-black smoke, away they sped.

Thankfully, it was almost two in the morning and there was nobody to knock over. But this didn't stop them tipping over a bin and scattering fish and chip bags all over the cobbled street.

'TURN LEFT!' bellowed Grandad.

Albert pulled the wheel over, scraping the wingmirror on a lamp post. 'Sorry,' he muttered.

In the back of the van, the monster

growled and howled. He was not enjoying the trip at all. But, then, nor was poor Albert.

Suddenly, there was a sharp, worrying 'CRACK!' from the back of the van. Oh no, thought Albert. The MegaSucker must be splitting, 'We must go faster,' he yelled to his grandad.

The old man nodded. 'Put your foot back on the clutch,' he told him confidently.

With a jittery nod, Albert felt for the pedal with his left foot and pushed it down. Grandad, in turn, slammed the van into second.

Flying over a hump-backed bridge,

the van lurched up the High Street, knocking over yet another bin, a post box and a perfectly parked green and yellow bicycle.

'PULL OVER!' the old man suddenly hollered, jabbing Albert in the ribs with his elbow.

Totally forgetting to push in the clutch, the boy slammed his foot on the brake. The van skidded to a halt, hiccuped twice and then, finally, juddered to a stop.

'The perfect spot to drop off a gigantic muffin monster,' chuckled Albert's grandad.

Albert looked out of his window to see where they were. Shocked, he turned back to the old man. 'Grandad! We can't.'

'Oh yes, we can.' He grinned wildly, showing Albert his two teeth. 'We don't want him to go hungry, do we?'

The boy frowned and slowly nodded. His grandad was crazy!

Jumping out of the van, Albert yanked open the back door. The MegaSucker, he saw, now had a big split in it and it was oozing green monster gunk. 'Hurry,' he panted, 'or he'll escape.'

The old man nodded and, together, they dragged the goo-smothered Hoover over to the door of Rufus Splinter's muffin shop.

Then the most horrifying thought hit Albert. How were they going to get the monster in there? Handing the metal cylinder to his grandad, he pushed frantically at the door, but it was bolted. Top and bottom! And so, he soon discovered, were all of the windows.

He looked over at his grandad who seemed to be having a lot of difficulty keeping hold of the jerking MegaSucker. 'What do we do now?' the boy whined.

Placing the Hoover down by his feet, the old man stretched and looked up. 'There.'

With a a nervy gulp, Albert followed

his grandad's gaze. He seemed to be looking at the roof of the muffin shop and at a big, fat chimney pot sitting on top of it.

Suddenly, Albert understood.

He felt a hand on his arm. 'I'm sorry, Albert. I'm too old to climb all the way up there. You must do it.'

The boy nodded grimly. 'Don't worry, Grandad. I'm good at gym. Top of the class.'

Out of the corner of his eye, Albert spotted a fire ladder running up the wall of the shop. Perfect! Wedging the trembling MegaSucker under his armpit, he began to scramble up the ladder to the roof. It was hard work and he almost slipped twice, but he kept on going.

Finally, he got to the top. Then, with all of his strength, he tossed the Hoover down the chimney.

It landed with a terrific bang, a cloud of black soot bellowing up from the chimney pot.

After rubbing the dust from his eyes, the boy sat perfectly still, listening. Then, after a second or two, a word, a wonderful, superb, truly magnificent word echoed up from the chimney. 'YUMMY!'

'WE DID IT!' Albert yelled down to his grandad. 'He's in there munching on Rufus Splinter's muffins.'

'Yipppppeeeeee!' howled the old man. He began to do a sort of jig in the street, his slippered feet twisting and twirling crazily. 'Now you just have to drive back,' he called up.

Chapter 9
What's in the Freezer?

THE NEXT MORNING, IT WAS VERY busy in Grandad's shop, lots and lots of customers pushing in the door to enjoy Grandad's tasty muffins.

'Well, I'm glad to see Magic Muffins is

open,' cackled a tiny woman, plodding into the shop. 'Rufus Splinter's Muffin Shop is all shut up.'

Grandad scratched his bobbly hat. 'How odd.'

'Yes, yes. A very funny carry on, I must say. I was standing there. It was well past 9 o'clock, that's when they always open, but the shop was all locked up. Well, I was very hungry so I hammered on the door but no answer. Then Rufus Splinter showed up in his red Ferrari. He looked terribly upset. He went in and there was lots of yelling and, well, munching.'

'Munching, you say,' murmured Grandad Irish with a thoughtful scowl.

But Albert saw his lips twitch.

Albert's grandad, for all his odd ways, was by far the best grandad in the world.

They still had lots and lots of customers but Albert spotted there were only two or three muffins left in the window.

'What'll we do?' he asked his grandad.

'Don't worry, lad.' The old man grinned wickedly. 'I did a spot of baking this morning when you were sleeping.' He turned to the next customer; a wrinkly woman in a yellow shawl. 'Back in a mo',' he told her. Then he led Albert down the corridor to the kitchen and, there, on the top of the oven stood a gigantic hill of strawberry muffins.

Suddenly, a thump, thump, thump echoed through the shop.

With a shudder, Albert turned to his grandad. 'There's not another monster in the cellar, is there?'

The old man shrugged, his skin ghostly-white.

Albert followed on his grandad's slippered-heels as he shuffled over to the cellar door. Gently, the old man pulled it open and, together, they crept down the steps.

THUMP!

THUMP!

THUMP!

'Over there,' whispered Grandad.

Slowly, they crept over to a big, long freezer. It was very old and speckled with rust and dirt.

A chunky-looking tool box sat on the lid. Together, Albert and his grandad picked it up and placed it on the floor. Then, slowly, little by little, they lifted up the freezer lid.

'IMELDA!' bellowed Grandad.

'GRANDMA!' yelled Albert.

Stepping gingerly out of the freezer, the old lady mustered up a grin. 'A bit nippy in there,' she joked.

Albert spotted it wasn't plugged in; a good job, he pondered, or she'd be a frozen lollipop.

Grandma was very bedraggled, her lacy, plum-red dress all crooked and splodged with dirt. But, oddly, she looked much fatter than when Albert had last seen her three months ago.

'I thought the critter'd gobbled you up,' puffed Grandad, hugging her tightly.

'No. No. Silly. Lucy worships me...'

Lucy, thought Albert. Wow! The monster was a she.

'...She thought I was her pet, bless her. So she put me in this freezer and fed me muffins every day.' Her eyes grew wary. 'Where is she now?'

Grandad told her where they had put the monster.

Looking gloomy, the old lady nodded. 'She was getting a bit big for the cellar,' she admitted.

'Well, there's lots of room in Rufus Splinter's muffin shop,' piped in Grandad, trying to cheer her up.

'And there's no way she'll go hungry,' added Albert.

Grandad gently tweaked Grandma's cheek. 'Let's go up to the kitchen and enjoy a big mug of hot milk.'

His wife nodded ardently. 'But no muffins. I'm sick of muffins.'

Albert and his grandad chuckled. 'No muffins,' they agreed.

Happily, they climbed the steps up to the kitchen. Grandad led the way followed by Albert and then Grandma. But when they got to the top, Albert discovered the old lady was no longer with them.

'Grandma!' he yelled down the cellar steps. 'Is everything okay?'

'Yes, yes,' she called back, hurrying up to him. She patted the boy on the shoulder. 'I was just, er - putting on my slippers.'

Watching the old lady scurry over to her husband, Albert scowled. Not surprisingly, there were no slippers on

her feet; and he knew why. They were
in her bedroom. He'd seen them when
he went to fetch the record player. So
why, he wondered, did Grandma just
tell him a big, fat fib.

Chapter 10

Grandma's Secret

THAT VERY NIGHT, WHEN GRANDAD
and Albert were tucked up in bed,
Grandma crept down the steps to the
dark cellar. Pulling the cord to switch
on the lamp, she walked over to the
most cobwebby corner of the room
where a big, wooden crate was

hidden in the shadows. She stopped and listened for a moment. Then, she knelt down and, slowly, pulled up the lid.

The old lady's wrinkly eyes sparkled with joy for there, curled up in the dirty straw, were two baby monsters.

TWINS!

With a whimper, they stretched and looked up.

'It's okay,' Grandma soothed them as they began to cry. 'It's only me. Here.' She placed a bowl in the straw next to them. 'Lots and lots of yummy muffins so you'll grow up big and strong.'

'Like mummy?' tweeted one of the baby monsters, stuffing a plum muffin in her fanged mouth.

Grandma nodded and pinched her pet's slimy cheek. 'Just like mummy,' she cooed.

THE END

Felicity Brady
and the
Wizard's
Bookshop

Billy Bob Buttons

book 1
GALIBRATH'S WILL

Felicity Brady
and the
Wizard's
Bookshop
Billy
Bob
Buttons
ook 2
ARTICULUS QUEST

I THINK I
MURDERED MISS

'Superb!
A laugh-out-loud gem - with a twist.'
Bookworm

BUS STOP

BY THE AWARD-WINNING
BILLY BOB BUTTONS

Billy Bob Buttons

Remember,
when you hunt assassins...
...trust nobody.

TOR

ASSASSIN HUNTER

Billy Bob Buttons

Evil needs only
a timid victim

TOR
WOLF RISING
book two of the TOR trilogy

by award-winning author
Billy Bob Buttons

The gripping story
of a magical legend

the GULLFOSS
legends